CARNA and the
Boots of Seven Strides

by Bill Harley

illustrated by David Schulz

To Connie, Barbara, Milbre,
Beth and Gwen —
the Blue Mountain storywomen

Published by Riverbank Press
801 94th Avenue North, St. Petersburg, Florida 33702

Copyright © 1994 by Riverbank Press,
a division of PAGES, Inc.

Printed in the United States of America

2 4 6 8 10 9 7 5 3 1

ISBN 0-87406-681-6

How *Carna and the Boots of Seven Strides* Became a Story

I wrote *Carna and the Boots of Seven Strides* as a story to be told out loud. While I still tell it, it's different from the stories I usually tell. Many of my stories are about things that happened to me, or things that might happen today. I wanted Carna to feel like a folktale, something that must have happened a long time ago, when magic seemed more possible.

I wrote the story thinking of my friend, storyteller Gwen Ledbetter, who was busy looking for stories with strong mothers in them. I had been reading some stories by Richard Kennedy, a favorite author of mine. One was about some strange boots that walked by themselves. One morning as I was lying in bed and just waking up, the phrase "boots of seven strides" came into my head—like a leftover dream. I like the number seven. Like the number three, it's found in many stories. "What would boots of seven strides do?" I asked myself. "Who would wear them?"

The story of Carna is my answer to the question. Just think, I was working while I was still in bed!

A story never stops growing as long as it is told. The story in this book is a little different from the way I told it three or four years ago, and different from the way I will tell it in another year. And if you tell it, you will make it your own, and it will be different from mine. But first, of course, you have to read it!

Happy reading!

—Bill Harley

CONTENTS

1

The Skin of the Brown Bull

Carna's mother was a strong woman with a gentle heart. She had raised Carna with love and patience, just as she had raised the thousands of plants that grew in her garden. She grew tomatoes and geraniums and marigolds, but that wasn't all. She also grew rubber plants from the jungles and sunflowers from the plains. She even grew a kind of plant that reindeer loved to eat. Carna's mother had raised all of these in the rich deep earth of her garden.

One morning, as Carna sat before her breakfast of steaming fresh bread, jam, and tea, her mother came to her.

"Go see your father," said her mother. "Ask him for the skin of the brown bull.

I want you to take it to the cobbler at the far edge of town. Tell him you are my daughter, and that you want him to make you Boots of Seven Strides. Not six, for six is not enough. Not eight, for eight is too many. Boots of Seven Strides."

"But what are they for?" asked Carna.

Her mother smiled. "You are growing up, and it is time for you to see the world and learn what is in your heart. Now go."

Carna found her father in the great old barn, where sunlight drifted through the cracks and stretched across the floor. Her father had rough, sure hands and kind blue eyes.

"Father," Carna said, "Mother sent me here for the skin of the brown bull. I am to take it to the cobbler for Boots of Seven Strides." She watched her father's face wrinkle into a smile. Then he reached up on the wall of the barn and took down a beautiful piece of tanned leather. To Carna, the leather seemed as big as the bull itself must have been.

He held it out. "Here you are," he said. "I have been saving this for you." He smiled at Carna, and she smiled back. Then she turned to go.

Carna walked slowly to town. The sun shined brightly, and the air smelled of spring and the wet earth. When she came to the cobbler's house, she walked up the brick path to the front door. A black cat with white paws lay curled in the sun on the mat. The door was bright red, and the door knocker was shaped like a man's fine boot. Carna set the leather down, then reached up to the knocker. She let it fall on the door once, then again.

A moment later, the door opened and the cobbler stood before her. He was tall and bent from leaning over his work table for years and years.

"My mother sent me with this," Carna said quickly. Her heart beat fast as she passed the skin of the brown bull to the cobbler. Before she could say more, the cobbler held up his hand to stop her from speaking.

"Come with me," he said, and waved Carna inside the house.

He led Carna through the front room and kitchen, then into his shop. Boots and shoes and pieces of leather filled every corner of the room. Sunlight fought its way inside from a small window. The boots and leather gave off a fresh, strong smell.

The cobbler held Carna's leather up to the light over his work bench.

"This is a fine piece of leather," he said. He looked at Carna's feet and asked, "How many strides are to be in these boots?"

"Seven," Carna said.

The cobbler nodded. "Seven is a good number," he said. "Come back in three days and you will have your Boots of Seven Strides."

Carna thanked the cobbler and said good-bye. As she left, she bit her lip to hold back the excitement she felt inside. Though Carna did not yet know just what the boots were for, she knew they were special.

"Boots of Seven Strides!" she said to herself as she skipped home.

Magical Boots

In three days, Carna returned to the cobbler's house. The cobbler led her to his front room. There, by the fireplace, she saw a beautiful pair of boots. They were the color of butterscotch and looked as if they would fit a large man.

"Are those your own boots?" asked Carna.

"No," laughed the cobbler, "they are your boots, your Boots of Seven Strides. Try them on."

Carna's heart sank. She was sure they were much too large. But she did as the cobbler said and pulled the boots on. To her surprise, they seemed to wrap snugly around her feet. She stood up

quickly and took a step forward. The
large boots buckled and she fell to her
knees.

"Ah," said the cobbler, "you need to
learn to walk again."

Carna took off the Boots of Seven Strides and put her old shoes back on. She carried the boots home, holding them tightly to her chest. Carna found her mother in the garden and knelt down on the ground among the rows of flowers. She showed her mother the butterscotch-colored boots.

"Put them on," her mother said. Carna removed her old shoes and pulled on the boots.

Her mother held Carna's chin gently in her hand. Carna looked into the warm gray of her mother's eyes, the color of a mockingbird's wings.

"Listen closely to me," said her mother. "Never put these boots on unless you know where you are going and why you are going there. And when you do put them on, you must speak these words, then say where you want to go. Listen."

Carna's mother spoke in a soft, sing-song voice:

"One stride for each direction—the south, east, west and north—

And then another for the earth that brings the living forth

One step more for all the sky, with moon and sun o'erhead

And last, one more to bring me home to sleep in my own bed."

Carna repeated the words over and over until she knew them by heart. Then she looked at her mother, eager to hear what would come next.

3

Practice, and then More Practice

"It is good that you know the verse well," said Carna's mother, "but there is much yet to learn. You must practice walking in the Boots of Seven Strides. Where do you want to go?"

"I don't know," said Carna.

"You must choose someplace, Carna," her mother whispered.

Carna looked toward the white gate in the front yard. It opened onto the road, and seemed to call her.

"To the gate," said Carna.

"Then walk to the gate," her mother said.

Carna stood up, her legs wobbling in the great boots that reached over her knees. She said the rhyme, and then said where she wanted to go. Carefully, she stepped forward. In seven strides, Carna walked across the yard to the gate. Then she turned and came back, once again in seven strides.

"Where next?" asked her mother.

"To the greenhouse," said Carna, as her eyes filled with wonder. As before, she recited the rhyme, then said where she wanted to go. In seven strides, Carna walked across the yard, behind the barn, and to her mother's greenhouse. Her strides were the largest, longest steps she had ever taken. Once again she walked back.

A smile spread across Carna's face, and she quickly sang out the rhyme.

"This time," she said more boldly, "I want to go to the oak tree on the other side of the field."

She took seven steps and crossed the open meadow to the oak tree, then returned.

"Now," said her mother, "you have your Boots of Seven Strides."

All that week, Carna practiced, each time saying the rhyme, saying where she wanted to go. Each time, she reached where she wanted to go in seven strides. Then she turned and came back, again in seven strides. Further and further she went each day, traveling on the roads and across the fields and through the forests she had known her whole life.

4

Time to Say Good-bye

One afternoon, Carna came home after a full day of traveling in the golden sunlight. Her parents sat in the front room with mugs of mint tea. Carna's heart filled with excitement as she stood before them.

"It's time for me to leave," she said. "I want to see the world."

Her father simply nodded, as if he had been expecting it. Her mother smiled and nodded too, but her eyes filled with tears.

The next morning, Carna packed the things she would need in her father's old pack. On the front steps, she pulled on the Boots of Seven Strides and stood up. Her parents watched from the door.

"Carna," her mother said, "travel around the world. Go as far as you can.

Look and listen carefully. When you have gone as far as you care to, and you learn what is in your heart, remember to come home again."

Her mother and father hugged her good-bye. Carna held her breath, and then said:

"One stride for each direction—the south, east, west and north—

And then another for the earth that brings the living forth

One step more for all the sky, with moon and sun o'erhead

And last, one more to bring me home to sleep in my own bed."

Carna waved good-bye to her parents. Then she faced the road and said, "Take me to the next village."

She stepped out of the yard, away from her home. Swallows circled around her and the wind sang in her ears as she walked down the road. Other travelers stopped and looked in wonder at the girl that strode by them. Carna's heart felt as large and open as the cloudless sky above her. She reached the next village by the end of the day, on her seventh stride.

The following day she traveled on. By noon of the third day she stood high on the hills that she had once seen in the distance from her house. Carna turned from the valley of her home and continued over the hills to the next country.

For weeks and weeks, Carna traveled on. Each day she decided where she wanted to go, sang the rhyme and traveled there in seven strides.

Sometimes Carna slept at an inn. Other times, she slept at the house of someone she had met along the way. Now and then, she slept out in the open, under the stars, awakening to find herself covered in a heavy, sweet-smelling dew.

As Carna traveled, stories about her spread. People talked of a girl in large boots who walked with the wind. Some said they had seen her. Some said they had only felt the breeze she made as she passed. People waved to her when they saw her. "Hello Carna!" they called. "How are your Boots of Seven Strides?"

5

A Strange Tale

One night, after walking many miles, Carna came to an inn and shared a meal with other travelers. After dinner, they sat back in their chairs and traded stories of their journeys. One tale followed another, each story finer than the one before. At last, it grew silent and all the travelers sat, alone in their own thoughts. Finally, one man who had not spoken all evening raised his voice.

"Ah, my friends," he said, "your stories are all wonderful, but I've been to a kingdom like no other. I'm glad to be back from it. For in that kingdom there lives a giant. It is a huge creature with three eyes. Two in the front and one in the back. And the one in the back is a terrible one. It never closes. With these three eyes, the giant can see you, no matter where you are. He comes out at night and walks the roads and countryside. One night, I heard him roaring and bellowing as he passed by where I was staying. Why, the whole earth shook."

"I've been to that kingdom," another traveler said, "but I left as soon as I could, for everyone who lives there is terrified. My heart broke to see people so afraid."

Everyone was silent. Carna felt something stir within her.

"What does the giant do?" she asked. "Does he eat people or destroy villages? What does he do if he finds people out at night?"

Both men shook their heads.

"I don't know," said the first man. "I never heard of anyone being caught. You see, all the villagers run inside and lock their doors at night. No one goes out till the morning."

"Where is this place?" asked Carna.

"It is far to the east, over the mountains that look like clouds," answered the man.

"Yes," added the second man, "it's so far, it seems like another world."

A breeze blew through the window by the table. A candle flickered, and the room was filled with the smell of lilacs and early summer. Carna knew where she wanted to go. She decided to start the next morning.

6

In the Land of the Giant

Carna was up with the sun. She had a large breakfast and put on her boots. She stood outside the door of the inn and spoke the rhyme.

"Take me to the mountains in the east," she called out.

In long, even strides, she walked toward the mountains more swiftly and surely than she had ever walked before. As she went, she saw the mountains grow larger and larger. On the seventh step that day, as the sun set behind her, she reached the foot of the great mountains. Night fell. The mountains turned dark, except for their tops, blanketed with snow that shone like a silver fire in the moonlight.

Carna slept well, then rose early the next morning. She spoke the rhyme and called for the boots to take her all the way up and over the mountains.

She felt the air grow colder as each stride brought her higher. Eagles circled above her, until she was so high that even they turned back to their homes in the forests below.

On the fourth step, she crossed over the tallest peaks. She looked down and saw a long green valley stretched before her. The valley was sprinkled with villages and farms, forests and roads.

Carna knew she must be near the kingdom, and that the giant could not be far now.

On her seventh step that day, she reached the valley and found herself in a deep grove of tall pines. She rolled out her blanket on the soft pine needles, with her head at the trunk of a huge tree.

As she fell asleep she thought to herself, "I am in the land of the giant!"

The next morning, Carna rose with her mother's words in her ears:

Never put these boots on unless you know where you are going.

Carna was not sure where she was going, so she wrapped up her Boots of Seven Strides, put them in her pack, and went barefoot. She walked until she came to a village. A man passed by her.

"Excuse me," Carna said, "but could you tell me about the giant that lives in this kingdom?"

The man's eyes grew wide. Instead of answering, he quickly walked away from her.

Carna walked on. After a while, she greeted a woman at work in a garden of petunias and snapdragons.

"Good morning, ma'am," Carna said politely.

The woman looked up and smiled. "Good morning, young lady," she answered.

43

"Could you tell me about the giant?" asked Carna. "I'd like to see him."

The woman's face darkened. She stood up quickly and gathered her basket and tools. "Foolish, foolish girl," she said. Then she turned and went into her house, closing the door behind her.

Wherever Carna went she met the same coldness and fear. The sky above the land stayed gray and lifeless, even at noon. In every village of the kingdom, people stared, spoke harshly to her and turned away when she asked about the giant.

"What is wrong with everyone here?" Carna asked herself. "How can they all be so afraid?"

7

Inside the Castle

Carna's journey continued. Days and nights passed so quickly that she could no longer keep track of them. How many days had she been gone? How many miles had she walked? How much farther would she have to go?

Finally, she came to the edge of the kingdom. In the heart of that kingdom there was a city, and there at the heart of the city was the castle of the king and queen. Carna stood before the castle, looking up at its great stone walls. She walked to the huge door and knocked. A guard looked down at Carna from the castle walls above her.

"What is your business?" demanded the guard.

"I am Carna," she answered, "of the Boots of Seven Strides. I wish to see the king and queen. I want to speak to them about the giant."

Minutes passed, and then the great door groaned open. The guard led Carna into the castle. She passed through long, dark hallways and into the throne room.

The room was lit by hundreds of torches. At the far end of the long room Carna could see the king seated on a throne of gold, and the queen on a throne of silver. Carna walked toward them.

The king looked at her and frowned.

"Little girl," he said, "who are you? Where is this Carna of the Boots of Seven Strides? Where is the hero who wants to speak to us about the giant?"

"I am she," said Carna.

The queen shook her head angrily and turned to the king. "This is just a girl," she said harshly. "This is no hero. And where are the Boots of Seven Strides? Look. She is barefoot. She is no help to us!"

"Take her out now!" the king ordered angrily.

The guard grabbed Carna by the collar and pulled her across the room. He dragged her through the halls of the castle and shoved her outside.

Carna sat on the street behind the castle and saw the sun set. People walked by, ignoring her. The great clock, high in the tower of the castle, struck seven. As the long, low tolls of the bell rang out across the city, people ran to their houses, scurrying like small animals. They shut the doors tightly behind them. Carna heard the sound of heavy bars sliding behind the doors. She saw the shades in all the houses being drawn. The city grew dark and the stars came out.

Carna sat alone in the streets of the kingdom's city, cold, tired, and far from home. She felt lonesome and alone.

Face to Face with the Giant

Suddenly, Carna felt the earth rumble and shake. The rumbling grew stronger and stronger. Then she heard the sound of footsteps, so heavy that even the walls of the castle shook. Off in the distance, she could see a dark shadow coming toward the city. She heard a roaring and bellowing along with the thundering footsteps.

The giant! It was a creature more horrible and fantastic than Carna had

imagined, even in her dreams. Closer
and closer the beast came, until he
reached the edge of the city. The giant
sat down on a small hill, put his head
in his hands and let out a long, sad
moan.

Carna reached into her pack and pulled out the Boots of Seven Strides. She sang the rhyme quickly, in time to her racing heart:

"One stride for each direction—the south, east, west and north—

And then another for the earth that brings the living forth.

One step more for all the sky, with moon and sun o'erhead

And last, one more to bring me home to sleep in my own bed."

"Take me to the giant!" Carna cried. In seven quick strides she walked through the streets of the city and reached the giant. She stood at the feet of the rough, huge creature.

"Hello," Carna called out bravely, "I have come to meet you."

The giant raised his head from his hands and saw the girl standing before him. He frowned.

"How did you get here?" he demanded roughly. "You could not have come from behind me."

Carna shrugged, even though her heart seemed to beat as loudly as the footsteps of the giant. "It doesn't matter how I've come," she answered. "Only that I'm here."

"But I see everything," the giant said. "I can see at night, and I see those who want to trick me." He laughed a horrible laugh. "I see them all, and no one can fool me."

"Your third eye is powerful," said Carna.

The look on the giant's face changed. He leaned forward and looked more closely at the girl before him.

Carna looked back. In the giant's eyes she saw not just anger and meanness. She saw a deep sadness.

"The power is a curse," the giant said softly. "For the eye will not close. Pain keeps me from closing the eye and I cannot sleep. I never sleep, and that is why I walk the roads at night."

The giant bowed his head and let out a sad sound that rolled across the dark countryside like distant thunder

"The eye makes you unhappy," Carna said. "Let me look at it. Perhaps there is something wrong with it."

But the giant suddenly grew fierce again. He let out a terrible bellow. "Stay away!" he roared. "I warn you! Stay away!"

9

Terrible Danger!

Carna knew what she must do. She called out her rhyme. "Take me to the top of the giant!" she cried to her boots.

Before he could know what she meant to do, Carna climbed to the giant's waist. Then she strained and pulled herself up until she reached his hair. It hung down around his shoulders like long, dirty ropes. Carna grabbed onto a tangled knot and began to pull herself up.

The giant roared. He reached back with both hands and tried to grab hold of her. He swung his head back and forth, trying to shake the girl loose. But Carna was too quick for him, and she held on, climbing until she reached the back of the giant's head.

She looked into the giant's eye. It was black and terrible. She saw the moon reflected in the dark eye, and then— something else. There, in the corner of the eye, was a branch of thorns. The branch was stuck so deep and so fast that it kept the eye from closing.

Still holding onto the giant's hair with one hand, Carna reached out for the branch with the other. She took a deep

breath, then pulled and pulled, until the branch of thorns came free and fell to the ground.

The giant screamed in pain. He rocked his head back and forth, back and forth.

Carna swung wildly, clinging to the giant's hair. As she fought to hang on, she thought of her mother. She remembered the way her mother had stood before their house, saying good-bye. She recalled her mother's words:

When you have gone as far as you care to, come home again.

Finally, the giant stopped roaring and swinging his head. Carna saw the large dark eye close and open again. The giant became quiet and still. Carna swung down on the giant's hair to his shoulder. The giant turned his head to the side and looked at her. Slowly, he put a hand to the back of his head.

"My eye . . . I can close it," the giant said softly. "Now, when it is closed, I can't see. What is behind me?"

Carna looked up at the face of the giant. His eyes searched hers for an answer.

"Nothing is there," answered Carna. "There is nothing there but your fears."

The giant let out a deep sigh. He lay down upon the hill and fell asleep. Carna climbed down from the giant and curled up beside him. She fell asleep, too.

10

The King and Queen Ask a Favor

The next morning, people found the giant asleep at the edge of the city, with Carna near him. As he woke up, they stood far away from him, afraid of what he might do.

He raised his head, groaned, and looked around. But he did not roar, and he did not try to harm anyone. The look in his eyes was not scary, but kind. The people saw they had nothing to fear.

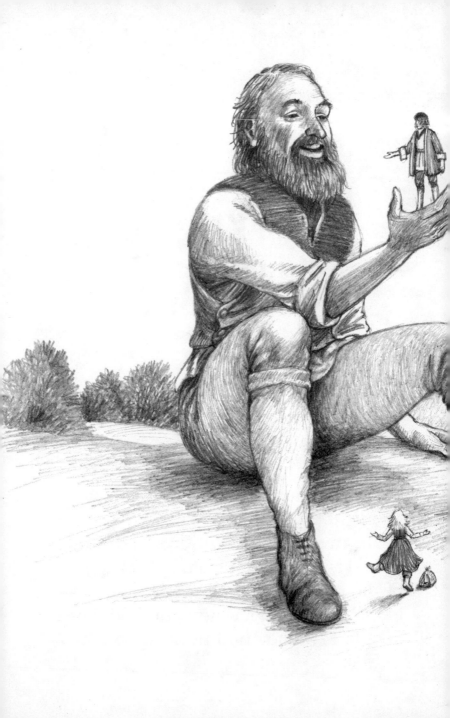

After a while, one man even crawled into the hand of the giant, who lifted the man high above the ground. Though the giant could have crushed him, he held the man gently and spoke kindly.

The story of Carna and the giant quickly spread throughout the kingdom. Soon the king and queen heard of what had happened. They called her to the castle. When she came into the throne room, the king and queen rose from their thrones and bowed before her.

"Please forgive us," the king said, "and accept our thanks. You have goodness in your soul, and courage and love for all in your heart."

Carna smiled. "I am glad I could help."

The queen put a hand on Carna's shoulder. "Carna," she said, "please stay here in our kingdom. Stay and be the guardian of the royal castle."

"Thank you for your offer," Carna said, "but I cannot stay. It is time for me to go home. Ask the giant. He will be your guardian."

Carna turned and walked out of the room, through the long, dark hallways of the castle. Once outside, she sat down

in the street and put on the Boots of Seven Strides.

Townspeople gathered around her as she stood, strong and sure in the boots that had brought her so far. "Good-bye, Carna. Good-bye and thanks!" they called out.

"Good-bye!" said Carna. Her heart filled with joy.

She spoke the rhyme her mother had taught her. Then she said, "Take me home."

Over many days and nights, and across the rest of the world, Carna made her way homeward. At the end of her seventh step, she reached the home she had left so long ago. She found her mother and father outside. Carna hugged her father. There were lines in his face, and streaks of silver shining in her mother's hair. How long had she been away?

"Carna, you have grown," said her
father. Carna saw that he was right. She
seemed to stand eye to eye with her
mother.

Carna's mother smiled and held her
tightly. "Where have you been? What
have you seen?" her mother asked.

"I've seen the world and found what
was in my heart, just as you told me to.
I've done things I never thought I could,"
Carna said.

She went to the garden and emptied her sack. Out of it poured seeds and dust and smells from around the world. There was nothing else in it.

Carna's mother gathered the seeds and began to plant them.

In the days that followed, Carna built her own home close to her parents' house. In it she built a huge fireplace, made of stones from the nearby fields. On the first night that she stayed there, a wintry wind blew down from the north. Carna built a large fire in the fireplace. The red flames roared and danced, warming the corners of the house. Carna smiled, pleased.

Then she took her Boots of Seven Strides, now scuffed and worn, and put them close to the fireplace. Carna decided to keep them there always, ready to travel, and ready to remind her of the world and all of the wonderful things in it.

One stride for each direction—the south, east, west and north—

And then another for the earth that brings the living forth

One step more for all the sky, with moon and sun o'erhead

And last, one more to bring me home to sleep in my own bed.

About the Author

Photo by Susan Wilson

Bill Harley is a professional storyteller and singer who has performed across the country nearly two thousand times since 1980. He is also known for his work on National Public Radio's "All Things Considered," and has been featured in several publications, including *Child* magazine, the *Christian Science Monitor,* the *Washington Post, Entertainment Weekly,* and *Booklist.*

Most of Bill's stories and songs are about everyday life, and a lot of them are about growing up. He has recorded many of his songs, including the popular "You're in Trouble," "50 Ways to Fool Your Mother," "Monsters in the Bathroom," "Grown-ups Are Strange," and "Dinosaurs Never Say Please"—all of which have received national awards.

Bill, who grew up in the Midwest, says he really had a very ordinary childhood. "I never spent much time in the principal's office, despite what some people might think. I behaved well enough that grown-ups just left me alone—so I held the adult world at arm's length. I still do."

Music became an important part of Bill's life when he was just a kid. He learned guitar, banjo, and piano and uses them when he performs. But education is important to him, too. He graduated from Hamilton College in New York with a degree in religion, and has made his interest in learning a lifelong experience that he likes to share. He has worked with the Rhode Island State Council on the Arts and the Massachusetts Arts Collaborative, and has led many workshops on storytelling and creative writing.

Bill lives in Seekonk, Massachusetts with his wife and two sons.

Carna and the Boots of Seven Strides is his first book.